Jack Frost's
Ice Castle

Goat Mountain

McKersey Castle

oom

The Great Cake Robbery

Goblins! Don your masks and dancing shoes,
It's time to celebrate—we've paid our dues.
The humans planned a costume ball,
But my icy magic will stop it all!

We'll crash the castle, steal their show,
Scatter costumes to and fro.
Of all my plans, this takes the cake,
I, Jack Frost, have chaos to make!

**Find the hidden letters in the masks
throughout this book. Unscramble all 7 letters
to spell a special dress-up word!**

Contents

McKersey Castle

"Rachel, look!" Kirsty Tate cried excitedly, pointing through the car window. "There's McKersey Castle!"

Rachel Walker, Kirsty's best friend, stared down the long driveway at the huge stone castle ahead. It was set on a hill, and it had two tall turrets, one on either side of the entrance gate.

"It's beautiful," Rachel breathed.

Mrs. Tate, who was driving, smiled in agreement. "Isn't it the perfect place for

a party?" she said. "It was so smart of Lindsay and Robert to choose a castle for their big costume ball." Lindsay was Kirsty's cousin, and she and her husband were celebrating their tenth wedding anniversary at McKersey Castle. Kirsty and her parents had been invited. Kirsty was allowed to bring a friend, so Rachel had traveled with the Tates all the way to the Scottish Highlands.

"It's a *masked* ball, too," Mr. Tate added.

"That'll be fun," Rachel said eagerly.

Kirsty nodded. "Wow!" she exclaimed as they got closer to the castle. "There's a moat and a drawbridge!"

"Just like a fairy-tale castle," Rachel said, smiling at Kirsty.

Kirsty grinned back at her friend. She and Rachel knew a lot about fairies, because they'd met them many times. In fact, the girls were now good friends with the fairies. That was Rachel and Kirsty's very special and magical secret!

The two girls watched with delight as the car crossed the drawbridge and came to a stop in the castle courtyard.

"Look at the battlements," Rachel said, pointing toward the top of the castle as she and Kirsty climbed out of the car. "I wonder if we're allowed to go up there."

"Hello!" cried Lindsay. Kirsty's cousin

rushed out of the large oak castle doors with her husband, Robert. She hugged the Tates one by one. "And you must be Rachel," Lindsay said, giving Rachel a hug, too. "Come inside, everyone."

"Is everything ready for the party tomorrow night?" Kirsty asked as they carried their bags toward the entrance hall.

"Not quite!" Lindsay replied. "The cake is coming today, and the party planning company that is organizing everything is delivering the costumes tomorrow. You'll be able to choose your outfits then."

"The other guests are arriving tomorrow, too," Robert added, as they stepped into the entrance hall.

The inside of the castle was cool and welcoming. There were tall arched windows, a flagstone floor, and a suit of armor standing in one corner. Colorful embroidered banners and tapestries hung from the ceiling.

"I've picked out a special bedroom for you two," Lindsay said to Kirsty and Rachel, as Robert led Mr. and Mrs. Tate to their room "Follow me." Lindsay led the girls up a winding staircase. "Ta-da!" she announced, throwing open a small wooden door. Rachel and Kirsty gasped with delight when they saw the huge room. It had two canopy beds and pretty white furniture. One side of the room was taken up with an enormous window. After the girls had put their bags down, they went to look out the window.

"We're right over the drawbridge!" Rachel cried excitedly.

"This used to be the old gatehouse,"
Lindsay explained.

"And where does that door by the
wardrobe lead?" asked Kirsty.

"Come and see," Lindsay replied.

The door opened onto another narrow

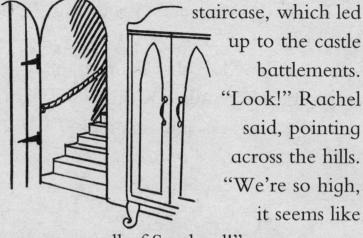

staircase, which led up to the castle battlements. "Look!" Rachel said, pointing across the hills. "We're so high, it seems like we can see all of Scotland!"

"I gave you that bedroom because I thought you two girls would be great at protecting the castle from intruders," Lindsay joked, her eyes twinkling. "I don't want anything to spoil this party!"

Suddenly, Kirsty spotted a white van approaching the drawbridge. "*McKersey Village Cakes*," she read from the side of the van.

"My cake!" Lindsay cried, hurrying over to the stairs. "I'm dying to see it! It was difficult to arrange, but a party's no good without a cake, right?" She grinned at them. "Be careful up here, OK?"

The girls nodded. "Lindsay's really excited, isn't she?" Kirsty laughed, as her cousin clattered off down the stairs.

"So am I!" Rachel said. She shivered. "Oh! Did you just feel that blast of icy wind, Kirsty?"

"Yes," Kirsty agreed, frowning.

Rachel's eyes widened. "I can see ice!" 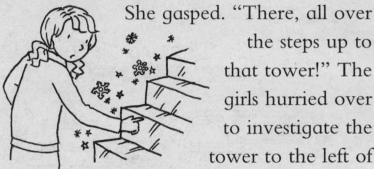 She gasped. "There, all over the steps up to that tower!" The girls hurried over to investigate the tower to the left of the drawbridge. Curiously, they began to climb the frozen steps. As they did, the air got colder and colder. Suddenly, Rachel and Kirsty heard a horribly familiar, icy voice.

"Raise my flag to the top of this tower!" it snapped.

Hardly daring to breathe, the two girls peeked around the tower wall to the top of the steps. To their shock, standing next to a gnarled green goblin, was Jack Frost himself!

Fairies to the Rescue

"Nothing will stop me from holding my Icicle Party here tomorrow night," Jack Frost declared, as his goblin struggled to unfold a flag. "Especially not a human costume party!"

Rachel and Kirsty glanced at each other in horror. Jack Frost was planning a party at the castle on the same night as Lindsay and Robert!

"This is the perfect place for my party," Jack Frost continued. "It's miles from anywhere!"

At last, the goblin managed to raise the flag to the top of the flagpole. As it unfurled, Rachel and Kirsty saw that it showed a picture of Jack Frost wearing a golden crown.

"Now we have to get rid of the humans," Jack Frost said coldly. "We will return to my ice castle immediately, and plan how to ruin this silly costume party before it's even started!" With a loud cackle, Jack Frost and the goblin zoomed away on a blast of icy wind.

"They're gone," Rachel said, relieved.

"But they'll be back!" Kirsty pointed out. "How are we going to stop them from ruining Lindsay and Robert's party?"

Rachel thought for a moment. "We could ask the fairies for help," she suggested. "We have lockets full of fairy dust to take us to Fairyland."

Kirsty nodded eagerly, as she and Rachel opened their lockets.

The girls sprinkled the glittering fairy dust over their heads. Immediately, they found themselves

tumbling through the air, shrinking to
fairy size and
surrounded
by dancing
rainbows.

As the rainbow
colors drifted
away, Rachel
and Kirsty floated
gently to the ground
outside the pink Fairyland palace.

"Should we knock on the door?"
Rachel asked. It was the first time
they'd ever arrived in Fairyland without
someone to meet them!

Kirsty nodded, so Rachel lifted the
butterfly-shaped door knocker and
tapped on the door.

Almost immediately, Bertram the frog footman hopped out. "Hello, girls!" he exclaimed, looking surprised. "Welcome back to Fairyland."

"Hello, Bertram," said Kirsty. "Could we see the king and queen, please?"

Bertram bowed, took a small silver bell off the table, and shook it.

"*Kirsty and Rachel to see the king and queen!*" sang out a chiming voice.

The girls listened in amazement as lots of bells tinkled inside the palace, passing on the same message from room to room.

"*The king and queen will see you now!*" a message came tinkling back.

"Follow me to the main chamber, please," said Bertram, leading the way.

The king and queen were sitting on their glittering golden thrones when Bertram and the girls arrived in the chamber. It was a large room with a domed ceiling studded with silver stars.

"This is a nice surprise," said King Oberon.

"Do you need our help, girls?" asked Queen Titania kindly.

"Your Majesty, Jack Frost is trying to ruin my cousin's party at McKersey

Castle tomorrow," Kirsty explained.
"He wants to hold his own
party there instead,"
added Rachel.
"We're holding our
annual costume ball here
at the palace tomorrow
night," Queen Titania
said, frowning.
"Maybe Jack Frost didn't
receive his invitation and
that's why he's throwing
his own party."
"Can you help us?"
asked Kirsty.
"Yes, we know just the fairy
for the job," declared the king.
The queen waved her wand, and

a cascade of multicolored sparkles streamed out of the open window.

A few moments later, a fairy flew in and landed gently on the marble floor. Rachel and Kirsty stared at her. The fairy was dressed  as Snow White! She wore a long red dress and carried a basket with an apple inside.

"This is Flora the Dress-up Fairy," said the queen.

"Hi, girls!" Flora beamed at them. "How can I help you?"

The girls quickly explained about Jack

Frost's awful plans to ruin Robert and
Lindsay's party. Flora shook her head,
looking annoyed.

"Don't worry," she said firmly, "we
won't let Jack Frost spoil the party!"

Goblin Trouble

"We can stop Jack Frost and those tricky goblins from ruining everything," Flora went on. "As long as they don't get ahold of my magic dress-up items!"

"What are they?" asked Kirsty.

"Flora's magic items change all the time," the queen explained. "Just like Flora's costumes!"

Flora nodded. "For Lindsay's party, my three magic items are a porcelain figurine in a princess gown, a Red Riding Hood cape, and a black mask with rainbow colored feathers," she told the girls. "The figurine will make the party food wonderful, the cape helps the costumes look good, and the mask ensures that all the guests have a great time."

"So if the goblins get those three magic things, will they be able to ruin Lindsay's party?" asked Kirsty nervously.

"Yes—but luckily, Jack Frost and the goblins don't know what they are!" Flora laughed. "Now, let's hurry to McKersey Castle and keep an eye on the party preparations. Just let me change my outfit."

Flora waved her wand over her head. A shower of turquoise and emerald sparkles drifted down around her. Rachel and Kirsty watched in amazement as the

fairy's long, curly hair became a tumble
of green and blue ringlets, topped with
a shell tiara. Flora's red dress became a

blue bandana
top and a
shimmering,
iridescent
turquoise skirt
that curved up into
a beautiful mermaid's
tail at her ankles.
"What a gorgeous
costume!" Kirsty gasped.
"Be sure to watch out for
any goblin tricks!" said the king, as the
queen lifted her wand to shower them
with fairy magic.

The girls and Flora nodded as they
were swept up in a cloud of fairy dust.

A moment later, they found themselves
back on the high walls of McKersey
Castle. Rachel and Kirsty were human-
size again!

Flora looked up at Jack Frost's
flag, frowned, and waved her wand.
Immediately, a stream of blue and green
sparkles surrounded the flag.
When they cleared, the
picture of Jack Frost had
vanished, and an L and
an R were intertwined
in curly pink letters — L for
Lindsay, and R for Robert! "That's
better!" Flora declared.

Rachel looked over the castle walls
at the courtyard below. The cake van
was parked there, with its back doors
open. But the next second she spotted

something else — goblins!

"There's a group of goblins around the cake van!" Rachel cried.

"The delivery man must be inside the castle with Lindsay," said Kirsty. "I hope he took the cake with him."

But as the girls and Flora watched, they saw three goblins climbing out

of the van. They were holding a large cardboard box. They began to tear it apart, revealing a beautiful three-tiered cake inside!

"The goblins have Lindsay's cake!" Kirsty said in dismay.

"And look," Rachel added, pointing at another van parked in the courtyard, with JACK FROST'S FROSTED DELIGHTS written on the side. "They're going to drive away with it!"

Cake Chaos

"We'll get down there more quickly if you're fairy-size, girls!" Flora said. With a wave of her wand and a sparkle of magic, Rachel and Kirsty were fairies again. Immediately, the three friends flew over the castle walls and hurried down to the courtyard.

"Oh no!" Flora exclaimed as they

hovered above the goblins. "My magic figurine is on top of the cake!"

Rachel and Kirsty looked closer. On top of the white and silver icing was a delicate porcelain figure wearing a flowing yellow dress.

"So if the goblins steal it, then *all* the party food will be spoiled?" Rachel asked in dismay.

Flora nodded, flying down to confront the goblins. Kirsty and Rachel were close behind.

"Put that cake down!" Flora demanded.

One of the goblins stuck out his tongue. "Go away, pesky fairies!" he jeered. "We're taking this cake to Jack Frost for *his* party."

Another goblin grabbed a chunk of icing from the cake and flung it at Flora and the girls. They had to dodge quickly out of the way!

The other goblins cackled with glee. They immediately started pulling off chunks of cake and hurling them toward Flora, Rachel, and Kirsty.

"Help!" Kirsty cried, as a large piece almost hit her.

"They're ruining the cake!" Rachel gasped.

Frowning, Flora lifted her wand. Suddenly, a swirl of magic sparkles sent a piece of the cake right back toward the goblin who'd thrown it. When it hit him in the mouth, he cringed. Then he licked his lips.

"Yum!" he declared. He pulled off

another lump of cake, but this time,
instead of hurling it at the girls, he
ate it.

"Greedy guts!" hollered the goblin
next to him. He stuffed a piece of cake
into his mouth, too.

"Leave some for us!" the other goblins
shouted. They all began gobbling
chunks of cake!

"Stop!" the biggest goblin shouted suddenly. "Jack Frost's waiting for us. We'd better put the cake in our van."

As the goblins struggled to load the messy cake into the back of their van, Flora, Rachel, and Kirsty tried to figure out what they could do to stop them.

JACK FROST'S FROSTED DELIGHTS

"Oh!" Rachel gasped suddenly. "They'll have to drive over the drawbridge to get out, won't they?"

Kirsty grinned, catching on. "If we lift the drawbridge up, they won't be able to leave!" she cried. "That's a great idea, Rachel!"

The goblins had piled into the van and were already driving off. Quickly, Flora pointed her wand at the drawbridge.

Emerald sparks shot toward the heavy chains that raised and lowered

the bridge, and very slowly, the
drawbridge began to rise.

"Look at the drawbridge!" squawked

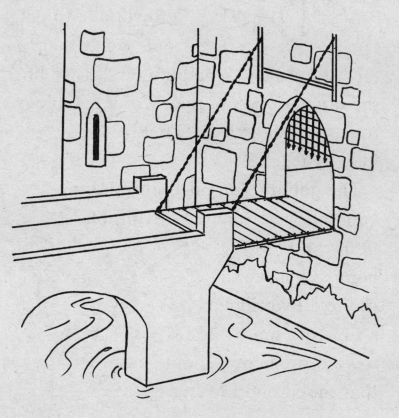

one of the goblins. "Go faster! We have to get out!"

The biggest goblin put his foot down on the gas pedal and the van lunged forward.

"It's no good!" Rachel cried. "The drawbridge isn't lifting fast enough!"

A Piece of Cake

As the van careened toward the rising
drawbridge, Flora flicked her wrist,
sending more fairy magic streaming
through the air. Rachel and Kirsty both
held their breath. As the goblins reached
the drawbridge, it swung swiftly up and
slammed closed, trapping the goblins'
van inside the castle.

"Thanks, Flora," Kirsty said. Flora winked at her, then waved her wand again and turned Rachel and Kirsty back to their human size. They all hurried over to the van.

"Now, give me my cousin's cake back," Kirsty said firmly. "Or Flora will send you all to the castle dungeons!"

The goblin in the driver's seat looked sulky. He muttered something under his breath. The next moment, the back doors of the van swung open. The goblins pushed the cake out onto the stone driveway. *Splat!*

Kirsty and Rachel looked at each other in dismay. The tiers of the cake had collapsed and the beautiful cake was completely ruined!

"Well, at least the magic figurine isn't broken," Kirsty said, picking it up carefully. "But everything else is a mess!"

"Now let us out of here!" the goblin driver yelled angrily.

Flora waved her wand again. With a creak, the drawbridge slowly lowered. The goblins immediately sped away. "Don't worry, girls, now that I've got the figurine back, I can fix the cake," Flora said. She grinned. "In fact, it will be a *piece of cake*!"

As she spoke, she sent a swirl of fairy magic in the direction of the ruined cake. The mess vanished in an instant. In the twinkling of an eye, a beautiful,

glittering *five*-tiered cake appeared, with
little arches holding up each layer. White
and pink iced flowers tumbled down the
sides of the cake. The magic figurine
was perched on top, and small figures in
costumes danced between the different
layers.

"Oh!" Kirsty breathed. "It's the most amazing cake I've ever seen!"

Rachel nodded in agreement as a cardboard box magically appeared and folded itself around the cake.

Just then, Lindsay and the delivery man came out into the courtyard. Flora darted into Kirsty's pocket just in time.

Looking excited, Lindsay opened the cake box. "Oh!" she exclaimed in awe. "What a *beautiful* cake! It turned out even better than I imagined!"

"It *is* pretty, isn't it?" Rachel said with a grin.

"Magical!" Lindsay sighed, and the girls exchanged a secret smile.

"You know, I was worried because everything in the kitchen today has been awful!" Lindsay went on. "The chefs were  getting all the recipes wrong, and the ovens weren't working properly. But this cake has made me feel a lot better!" She turned to the delivery man. "Could you help me carry it inside, please?"

"Everything will be fine in the kitchen now that the magic figurine is back, girls," Flora whispered, flying out of Kirsty's pocket. "Thank goodness," Rachel said.

"I need to return to Fairyland," Flora went on, "but I'll be back — and so will Jack Frost's goblins. Be on the lookout!" With that, she blew the girls a kiss and vanished.

Rachel and Kirsty smiled at each other, determined. They'd saved Flora's magic figurine so the party food wouldn't be ruined, but what tricks were Jack Frost's goblins going to try next?

The Big Costume
Kidnap

Contents

Colorful Costumes

"Jack Frost must be annoyed that his goblins didn't get away with the cake!" Rachel said to Kirsty with a smile.

It was the following morning and the girls were walking downstairs into the entrance hall of the castle. Sunshine streamed in through the arched windows, and everyone was bustling around, busy with final preparations for the party that evening.

"Yes, so we *have to* keep a lookout for more goblin mischief today," Kirsty replied. Lindsay hurried by, carrying a vase of flowers. "We don't have to get ready for the party for a while, so we could ask Lindsay if there's anything we can do."

"Good idea," Rachel agreed.

The two girls went over to Lindsay.

"Can we help?" asked Kirsty.

"Oh, thank you!" Lindsay said
gratefully, placing
the flowers on
a table. "The
costumes arrived
an hour ago and
they're up in one
of the bedrooms.
Do you think
you could check
and make sure
that all the outfits
have the right accessories with them?"

The girls nodded, so Lindsay led them
quickly toward one of the bedrooms on
the second floor.

"Most of the guests will be arriving

in the next couple of hours," Lindsay explained. "They'll be coming to choose their costumes then, but you two can have first pick. They're all in here." She stopped outside a heavy wooden door.

"*Hee hee hee!*" Kirsty jumped as she heard a muffled giggle coming from inside the room. Unfortunately, she knew exactly who giggled like that— goblins! She glanced at Rachel and Lindsay. Kirsty could tell from Rachel's face that she'd heard it, too, but luckily Lindsay hadn't noticed.

"So," Rachel said quickly, stepping in front of Lindsay so that she didn't open the door, "you want us to check that all the costumes are correctly displayed?"

"Yes," Lindsay replied. "Just make sure that Robin Hood has his bow and arrows, that kind of thing."

"We'll be fine, Lindsay," Kirsty told her. "You can leave it to us. You must have a lot to do!"

"Oh yes," Lindsay agreed. "I have to check on the decorations in the ballroom

now. Thank you, girls." She
hurried off.

"Watch out for goblins!"
Kirsty whispered to
Rachel as she
opened the door.

Rachel groaned
as the door swung
inward. Two
giggling goblins
were pulling
costumes off the
racks.

The room was
a complete mess!

One rack of
costumes had been completely knocked
over. In the middle of the room there

was a huge, messy heap of clothes. When the goblins saw the girls, they started grabbing armfuls of brightly colored costumes from the pile and throwing them out the window. "Stop that!" Rachel cried. The goblins each gathered another armful of clothes and then climbed onto the windowsill. "They're going to jump!" Kirsty shouted. As she and Rachel ran across the

63

room, the goblins leaped out of the window, holding onto a thick, heavy rope. The girls saw that the rope had been tied to one of the wardrobes in the room, and the other end dangled out the window. The goblins were making their

escape by lowering themselves down the castle wall, holding onto the rope.

"Look!" Kirsty cried, pointing down at the moat.

A rowboat bobbed gently in the water. Three more goblins sat in the

boat, surrounded by all the stolen
costumes, hats, and shoes that the two
goblins had thrown out the window.

Kirsty's heart sank as she spotted

a bright red hooded cape on top of the pile. It was shimmering with fairy magic.

"Oh no!" she gasped, pointing it out to Rachel. "They have Flora's magic Red Riding Hood cape!"

Boat on the Moat

"Let's get down there!" Kirsty replied, running for the door with Rachel at her heels. "It's too bad that Flora isn't here to turn us into fairies!"

The girls dashed down the stairs and into the entrance hall, which was now empty. Suddenly, the visor in the suit of armor in the corner snapped open.

"Hello, girls!" called a voice, and Flora darted out of the visor. "Where are you going in such a hurry?" Rachel and Kirsty slowed down. "The goblins stole half of the dress-up costumes, including your magic cape!" Rachel explained. "And they're about to escape across the moat!"

"We've got to stop them!" Flora exclaimed.

She and the girls raced out of the hall, through the courtyard, and onto the drawbridge.

"There they are!" Kirsty yelled,
pointing.

The goblins were rowing furiously
away from the drawbridge, toward the
bend in the moat. As they disappeared

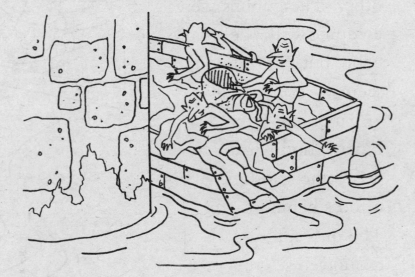

around the side of the castle, Rachel
turned to Flora. "We have to stop them
from getting away!" she cried.

But Flora shook her head. "Don't worry, girls," she replied calmly. "Just wait here."

Confused, Rachel and Kirsty glanced at each other. The goblins were escaping with the magic cape, but Flora didn't seem worried at all!

A moment later, Rachel and Kirsty heard the splashing of oars behind them. The girls spun around to see the silly goblins rowing toward them from the other side of the castle.

"The goblins have gone around in a circle!" Kirsty laughed. "They didn't realize that the moat makes a big circle around the castle."

Rachel and Flora grinned.

"Hey!" one of the goblins screeched suddenly. "There's the drawbridge. We're back where we started!"

"This is all your fault!" yelled another goblin, glaring at the two who were rowing the boat. "I'm going to throw you into the moat, and the alligators will eat you!"

"I'm not scared of alligators!" shouted
one of the rowers. Then he paused.
"Um, what's an alligator, anyway?"

"I know what an alligator is," said one
of the other goblins importantly. "It's
pink and it has eight legs!"

"No, that's not an alligator," the
first goblin yelled angrily. "That's an
elephant!"

The goblins
began to push
and poke
each other
as they
argued. The
two who
were rowing
dropped their oars and joined in, and the

boat began to drift aimlessly toward the drawbridge.

"Maybe we can lean over and grab the magic cape," Rachel whispered as the boat approached.

"Especially since the goblins are arguing too much to notice us," added Kirsty.

"Good idea." Flora nodded. "Let's go for it!"

Goblins Get Dressed

Rachel and Kirsty laid down on the
drawbridge and dangled their arms over
the water as the boat came closer. But
just as Rachel reached out her hand to
snatch the sparkling red cape, one of the
goblins looked up and spotted them.

"They're trying to steal our costumes!"
he yelled, grabbing one of the oars. "Get

away from the drawbridge! Row for the bank!"

Rachel, Kirsty, and Flora watched in disappointment as the goblins rowed away as fast as they could.

"I almost got the cape, too," Rachel groaned, scrambling to her feet.

Once the goblins reached the bank, they began throwing the costumes out of the boat and onto the grass. Then they jumped out of the boat themselves. As Rachel, Kirsty, and Flora rushed across the drawbridge,

they heard the goblins
yelling at each other.
"There are too
many costumes
for us to
carry!" one
shouted. "What
should we do?"

"Put some of the clothes on!" hollered
another goblin, struggling to get into
a pair of red velvet pants. He put a
white curly wig on his head,
and then a sailor's hat on top
of that. "We can just carry
the rest!" the goblin decided.

As Flora and the girls
hurried toward the bank,
they watched in
amazement as the goblins

dressed themselves up. One put on
a tiger outfit with a tail, and
then added a sparkly vest,
a red clown nose, and three
hats, including
a straw one with
a plastic flower
on it. Another
goblin was
wearing a pink
clown wig
with
a golden
crown on
top. He also
had the magic
cape slung around
his neck, but the hood
kept falling forward over his face.

Because the costumes were human-size, they were much too big for the goblins. They all had mismatched shoes that didn't fit, and kept tripping as they rushed around scooping up the rest of the outfits. Flora, Rachel, and Kirsty couldn't help laughing as they reached the bank. "Hand over those costumes!" Flora called. "No!" shouted the goblin with the cape. "Jack Frost's holding his party here tonight, so you won't be needing these!"

His friends cackled gleefully. Then one of them picked up a long princess gown and threw it right over Rachel

and Kirsty. Flora was fluttering alongside the girls and got trapped under the dress, too.

"Help!" Rachel cried.

"Everything's dark!" Kirsty gasped.

Goblins Meet Goats

As the girls and Flora struggled to free themselves from the heavy dress, they heard the goblins rushing away.

"We have to catch them!" Rachel panted as she and Kirsty finally managed to throw off the dress.

"Look, they left some of the costumes behind," said Kirsty, pointing at a heap of clothes on the grass.

Rachel looked
worried. "We
can't leave them
here in case
Lindsay finds
them," she said,

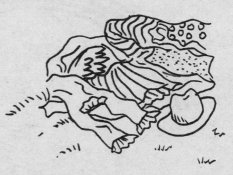

picking up an embroidered jacket. "But
we can't carry them while we run after
the goblins, either."

Kirsty frowned as she looked
more closely at the jacket
Rachel was holding.
"The sleeves are almost
falling off!" she
exclaimed, pointing
at the jacket.

"Look, the stitches are loose."
"That's because the magic cape is

missing," Flora explained. "The costumes are starting to fall apart at the seams."

"Oh no!" Rachel sighed. "The party will be ruined if we don't get the cape back soon."

Kirsty turned to Flora. "Flora, could you shrink the costumes?" she asked eagerly. "Then they'd fit into our pockets!"

"Sure!" Flora laughed and waved her wand.

After a swirl of fairy dust, a neat pile of tiny clothes, shoes, and

hats lay on the bank. Rachel and Kirsty kneeled down and carefully filled their pockets. Then they raced across the hills after the goblins!

Luckily, Flora and the girls could see the magic cape shimmering ahead of them in the distance, so they could easily keep track of where the goblins were going.

"Look, there's a cowboy hat," Rachel

 said, scooping up a hat that was lying on the grass.

"And there's a pink clown wig," Kirsty added, pointing a little further ahead. "The goblins must have dropped them."

Quickly, Flora shrunk the hat and the wig so the girls could fit them into their pockets. Then they hurried after the goblins, picking up other dress-up items that the goblins had dropped along the way.

A little bit farther on, Kirsty stopped

and shaded her eyes, peering ahead to see where the goblins were.  She saw them climbing a steep slope, toward a herd of mountain goats. That gave Kirsty an idea.

"Somehow we have to get the goblins to stop so that we can catch up!" Kirsty said urgently to Flora. "Do you think you could use your magic to ask those goats to help us?"

"What a great idea!" Flora beamed. She pointed her wand at the goats. A stream of green and blue bubbles floated through the air toward the herd. The bubbles hovered next to the goats' ears and then burst gently, making little bleating sounds.

"*Bleat! Bleat!*"

"That's goat language," Flora
explained, as Rachel and Kirsty smiled.

The goats looked up from the
grass they had been eating. Then, as
Flora and the girls watched, all the
goats trotted over to stand in front of

the goblins, blocking their path.

The goblins skidded to a halt and stared nervously at the hairy creatures. Flora, Rachel, and Kirsty hurried to catch up. As they got closer, they could see the goblins shaking with fear.

"Are these alligators?" one asked fearfully.

"No," said the one with the cape.
"I think they might be Pogwurzels!"

"*Pogwurzels?*" the others chorused in alarm.

"Yes. And we all know that Pogwurzels eat goblins!" wailed the one with the cape.

All the goblins shrieked with terror as one of the goats trotted forward. It leaned over to sniff the plastic flower on one goblin's straw hat. "Please don't eat me, Mr. Pogwurzel!" the goblin begged, too frightened to move.

"He looks hungry!" Rachel called, although she was secretly very sure that goats didn't eat goblins.

"Maybe they want to eat the clothes," shouted Kirsty, as another goat sniffed at a goblin's sleeve.

Immediately, all the goblins threw down the clothes they were carrying. The goats sniffed curiously at the costumes but then turned their attention back to the goblins. With shrieks of fear, the goblins quickly  pulled off all the dress-up clothes they were wearing.

"We're sorry, Mr. Pogwurzel!" the one with the tiger costume cried.

"We didn't mean to disturb you!" another goblin yelped. He placed his wig carefully at the goats' feet.

The one with the magic cape took that
off last. "Don't eat me, Mr. Pogwurzel!"
he begged, holding the cape out toward
one of the goats. "This cape is much
tastier than I am."

The goat snorted, which was too much for the goblin. He squealed with fright, threw the cape on the ground, and fled, with his goblin friends charging after him.

Costume Cleanup

Flora, Rachel, and Kirsty giggled.

"The goats won't really eat the costumes, will they?" Kirsty asked anxiously as the goats sniffed at the pile of clothes.

Flora shook her head. She shrank all the costumes, including the magic cape, so that the girls could gather them up in their pockets. "Goats like young thistle plants best of all," she said. And with another wave of her wand, she turned a large patch of purple heather into a field of thistles. The goats immediately bent their heads, took a sniff, and began to stuff themselves on thistles.

"Thank you, goats!" called Flora and the girls as they set off back to McKersey Castle.

"Weren't the goblins silly?" Rachel laughed as they hurried back across the drawbridge.

Kirsty nodded. "And they did look

funny wearing all those costumes," she added.

Soon they were back in the room where the dress-up costumes were stored. The girls looked dismayed as they glanced around.

"I'd forgotten how much of a mess the goblins had made!" Kirsty sighed, staring at the overturned rack and the costumes lying everywhere. "How are we going to get this all cleaned up before Lindsay comes back?"

"No problem!" Flora announced cheerfully. "Leave it to me."

The little fairy danced around the room, flicking her wand here and there, and sending little puffs of magical fairy dust whirling down onto the costumes. Rachel and Kirsty watched in delight as the clothes lifted off the floor and floated in the air. They danced over to the racks, their sleeves waving happily. The hats and wigs bobbed through the air, too, and all the shoes began to tap-dance

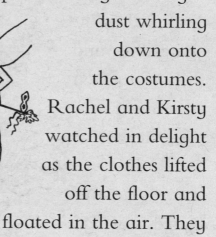

over to join
their costumes.
"Look!" Rachel said
to Kirsty. "All
the clothes, hats,
and shoes are sorting themselves
into the right outfits!"

Kirsty nodded as the curly pink wig
drifted past to join the red nose, striped
pants, and enormous shoes of the clown
costume.

Then the tiny clothes
began floating out
of the girls'
pockets. As
they danced through
the air, the costumes
grew back to their
normal sizes before

finding their places on the racks. Rachel even noticed that, now that the magic cape was safe and sound, the sleeves on the embroidered jacket weren't loose anymore.

"This is amazing, Flora!" Kirsty exclaimed as the last few pieces of the costumes moved into place. "Look at this, Rachel. All the men's costumes are here and the women's costumes are on this rack here."

"And the animal costumes are on a separate rack," Rachel added, pointing to where the striped tiger costume was hanging. "Thank you so much, Flora. All the costumes look perfect!"

Flora beamed at them. "You've got one item left in your pocket, Kirsty," she said. As she spoke, the magic red cape floated out. "I want someone special to wear it," Flora said thoughtfully. "Let me see . . . a-ha!" Her face lit up and she lifted her wand. Immediately, the Red Riding Hood dress and basket lifted themselves off the rack and floated over to settle on a chair. The magic cape drifted over to join them, growing back to its normal size along the way. Last of all, a big white label appeared in a burst of magic sparkles and pinned itself to the cape.

"*Mrs. Tate,*" Kirsty read out loud. "Rachel, that costume's for my mom!"

With a gleam in her eyes, Flora tapped her wand on the chair. A furry gray wolf costume instantly appeared, with a label that said MR. TATE. Kirsty and Rachel

burst out laughing.

"That's fantastic, Flora!" Kirsty said gratefully. "Thank you so much."

"And thank *you*, girls," Flora said with a wide smile. "But don't forget that Jack Frost will still be doing his absolute best to stop the party from happening.

Or, should I say, his absolute *worst!*"

Kirsty and Rachel nodded.

"We'll be careful," Rachel promised.

"Now I must go back to Fairyland, and you two had better choose yourselves some costumes," Flora said with a wink. "I'm sure that you'll find the *perfect* outfits if you look hard enough!"

As Rachel and Kirsty waved good-bye, the little fairy disappeared in a colorful swirl of glittering fairy magic.

The Magic Mask Mystery

Contents

Lindsay's Angels

"Hello, girls!" The door opened and Lindsay came in. "Wow! You've done a *great* job with the costumes!" she declared, looking around.

Rachel and Kirsty smiled. Flora had finished tidying up the room with her magic just in time.

"Have you chosen your outfits yet?" Lindsay asked.

Rachel and Kirsty glanced at each other excitedly. Flora had said that she was sure they'd find the perfect dress-up costumes. Had she used her fairy magic to leave special outfits just for them?

Kirsty's face lit up as she noticed a few blue and green sparkles floating around one of the racks. "Actually, we were just about to take a look," she said, nudging Rachel.

Rachel spotted the sparkles, too.

Together, the two girls hurried over to the rack. Hanging at one end, they found two beautiful angel costumes. The dainty white dresses sparkled with a silver sheen. There were even matching feathery wings, delicate halos, and silver cardboard angel harps. White feather masks glittering with silver sparkles completed the outfits. Rachel and Kirsty looked at each other in delight as they took the gorgeous costumes off the rack.

"We'd *love* to wear these outfits," Kirsty said to Lindsay. "I don't even remember seeing those," Lindsay said with a smile, "but they *are* beautiful. They'll be perfect for you two!"

They all turned around as the door opened again. Mr. and Mrs. Tate came in, followed by several couples.

"All the guests are here now, so we're bringing them in to choose their costumes," Mrs. Tate explained.

Lindsay smiled at everyone. "Why don't you go and change?" she said to the girls. "Then you can go and take a peek at the ballroom decorations."

Rachel and Kirsty nodded happily.

"Mom, Dad," Kirsty called as she headed for the door with her angel outfit. "Your costumes are on the chair."

Mr. and Mrs. Tate laughed when they saw the Red Riding Hood and wolf costumes. Rachel and Kirsty shared a smile as they hurried off to their room to change clothes.

"I'll help you do your hair, and then you can help me with mine," Kirsty said as they slipped the pretty white dresses on. "Then we can put the halos on top."

"Don't our costumes look fantastic?" Rachel gushed as they stood side by side admiring themselves in the mirror.

"Yes, thanks to Flora," Kirsty agreed happily.

"Let's go downstairs and look at the

ballroom," suggested Rachel. "The party will be starting soon. I can't wait!"

Carrying their harps, the girls went downstairs to the enormous ballroom. The doors were open, so Rachel and Kirsty peeked inside. All the other guests were still getting dressed, so the room was empty.

"Isn't it beautiful?" Kirsty whispered.

The ballroom was decorated in white and gold. There were long white curtains held back by twisted golden ropes at the

windows, glittering crystal chandeliers hanging from the ceiling, and sprays of white roses on all the tables. There were also white marble statues placed around the room wearing beautiful masks.

"I don't think any of those masks are Flora's magic one," remarked Rachel. "Don't forget that we have to make sure

the goblins don't get ahold of it, Kirsty,
or the party will be ruined!"

Kirsty nodded. "There's the cake,"
she said, pointing to a table at the
other end of the room. The girls placed
their harps on the table as they went to
take a closer look.

"The cake looks even more beautiful here in the ballroom," Rachel said with admiration.

But Kirsty was distracted by a blue-and-emerald figurine on the cake's middle tier. "Look!" she exclaimed. "That figure looks just like Flora!"

"Yes, it does," Rachel agreed.

Suddenly, the figurine winked at them! Rachel and Kirsty were so startled, they almost knocked their harps off the table.

"It *is* Flora!" Kirsty laughed.

"Hello," called Flora, fluttering over to the girls with a big smile.

Before Rachel could reply, a movement in the courtyard caught her eye. She glanced out the window and saw a group of odd-looking guests. They were very short and had extremely large feet.

"Goblins!" Rachel gasped in dismay. "They're arriving for Jack Frost's party!"

Goblin Guests

"We have to stop them!" Flora said. The three friends rushed out of the ballroom.

There were five goblins outside, all dressed in top hats and tails. They were heading toward the entrance hall door as Flora, Rachel, and Kirsty emerged in the courtyard.

"Hello!" Rachel called quickly. "Are you coming to Lindsay and Robert's party?"

"No!" snapped one of the goblins. "We're going to *Jack Frost's* party!"

"Oh, that's not *here*," Kirsty said. "I assume it will be at his ice castle."

Muttering grumpily, the goblin pulled out a large invitation. "It says here that Jack Frost's party is taking place at McKersey Castle!" he said loudly.

The girls glanced nervously at Flora, who had ducked behind one of Kirsty's angel wings. The little fairy grinned and aimed her wand at the invitation. A few magic sparkles went zooming toward it.

"Tell him to check again!" she
whispered to Kirsty.

"Are you sure you haven't made
a mistake?" Kirsty asked the goblin.

"Of course!" the
goblin said rudely,
shoving the
invitation under
the girls' noses.
"It says—" But
then he stopped.
His eyes almost
popped out of his head as they all
read the swirly, silver writing: *Jack Frost's
ice castle.*

"The party *is* at Jack Frost's ice castle!"
the goblin mumbled sheepishly.

The other goblins looked confused.

Muttering angrily, they all turned around and slunk away. "And tell your friends," Kirsty called after them, "that Jack Frost won't be happy if his guests are late!"

"Good!" Flora said with satisfaction, hiding on Kirsty's shoulder as the girls went back inside. "That will keep some of the goblin guests away."

Inside the entrance hall, people were gathering for the start of Lindsay's party. Rachel and Kirsty smiled to see a man dressed as a scarecrow. He was standing rigidly in the corner with his arms straight out to the sides.

"He's acting just like a real
scarecrow!" Rachel whispered to Kirsty.
"Isn't that funny?"

Kirsty nodded as
a man in a
cowboy outfit
strolled toward
them. "Howdy,
girls," he drawled,
tipping his hat.

Rachel and
Kirsty couldn't help
laughing.

"*Grrr!*"

Startled by the sound of growling, the
girls looked around. A woman dressed in
a tiger outfit was staring at them. Then

she sprang forward—and Rachel and
Kirsty had to jump out of the way!

"She's taking her costume a little
seriously!" Rachel whispered as the tiger
woman began "sharpening" her claws.

Just then, Lindsay rushed into the entrance hall. She wasn't wearing her costume . . . and she looked very upset.

"What's the matter, Lindsay?" asked Kirsty anxiously.

"My mask is missing!" Lindsay said. "I don't know where it could be. It's a complete mystery! The mask is black with rainbow colored feathers. Have you seen it?"

Rachel and Kirsty shook their heads, glancing at each other in dismay. They recognized the description: It was Flora's magic mask!

"The goblins must have stolen my mask," Flora whispered, as Lindsay hurried around the entrance hall, asking the other guests if they had seen it.

"Is that why the guests are behaving so strangely?" Kirsty asked.

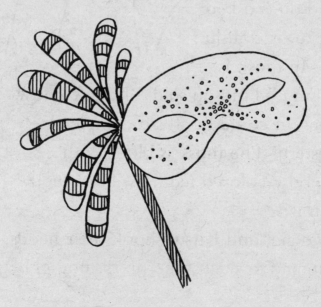

Flora nodded. "Yes," she said anxiously. "The fairy magic in your lockets must be protecting you two, but I think the other guests are turning into their costume's characters!"

Missing Mask

"Oh no!" Rachel whispered to Kirsty. "Remember all those crazy costumes we sorted through? We have to find the magic mask, or this party will be chaos!"

"Lindsay, we'll help you look," Kirsty called to her cousin. "Where did you last have your mask?"

Lindsay frowned. "I had it in the

ballroom," she said slowly, "and I took it to the wine cellar when I went to get a bottle of champagne."

"We'll look in the cellar while you search the ballroom," Rachel suggested.

Lindsay nodded. "Thanks, girls."

The entrance to the wine cellar wasn't far from the entrance hall. Rachel and Kirsty climbed down the staircase and began to look around. "What's that?" Kirsty asked, pointing to the flagstones on the ground.

There was a fine layer of dust on the floor, and the girls and Flora could see footprints. Next to them lay a tiny pink feather.

"That's a feather from my magic mask!" Flora exclaimed. "And those are goblin footprints! Let's follow them."

The footprints led to a wall at the back of the cellar, where they stopped abruptly.

"Did the goblins use Jack Frost's magic to walk through the wall?" Kirsty wondered out loud.

The girls peered closely at the wall and moved their hands over it carefully.

"I can feel a draft here!" Rachel said excitedly, with her hand on the space between two stones.

"A secret door!" Flora exclaimed.

Just then, Rachel noticed a smooth, round indentation in one of the stones. She pressed it and immediately the wall began to swing back. Rachel, Kirsty, and Flora stared at the dark passageway  that stretched away behind the wall.

"The goblins must have escaped down this secret passage with the mask," Kirsty said.

"I wonder where it goes," Rachel replied. "It's too dark to see." She looked nervous. "Jack Frost and his goblins might be hiding in there!"

Immediately, Flora waved her wand and the tip began to glow with a bright light. Now Rachel and Kirsty could see into the passage ahead.

The three friends crept down the narrow hall until they found themselves face to face with another stone wall.

"Oh!" Rachel said in disappointment. "It's a dead end."

"Maybe not," Kirsty replied. She ran her hands over the stones and found a round indentation just like the one that had opened the other wall. Kirsty pressed it, and the wall began to move. "Don't open it all the way, Kirsty," Flora whispered. "We don't know what's on the other side!"

Quickly, Kirsty took her finger off the

indentation, so that the wall stayed open just a crack.

The girls and Flora peered through the narrow opening. Behind it was not a hallway, but a cavelike room instead. They could hear a familiar voice. . . .

"Now listen to me, goblins!" it was saying. "I'm going to tell you *exactly* how to ruin this pesky party!"

"Oh no!" Kirsty whispered. "It's Jack Frost!"

Jack Frost Unmasked!

"I want you to steal every mask in the castle!" Jack Frost declared gleefully, sitting in a big chair before his goblins. His back was to the girls. "And cause as much trouble as you can, while you're doing it. We have to get these annoying humans out of the castle!"

"Look at the mask in Jack Frost's hand," Rachel breathed.

Kirsty and Flora stared at the mask. It was black with rainbow colored feathers, and it shimmered slightly with magic.

"It's my magic mask," Flora said softly.

"I'm going to wear *this* mask because it's the best one, and I'm the most

important person!" Jack Frost boasted, waving it in the air.

"He doesn't realize it's the magic mask," Flora said to Rachel and Kirsty.

"But how are we going to get it away from him?" Rachel asked.

"He's very close," Kirsty pointed out. "Maybe I can just grab the mask and we can make a run for it?"

"Let's try," Flora agreed. "Once we have the mask, I'll use my magic to block the entrance to the secret passage so that you can escape."

Kirsty felt extremely nervous as she edged her way carefully through the gap. She hoped the goblins wouldn't spot her! Luckily, she was hidden by Jack Frost's chair.

"Now make sure every human in this

castle is gone as soon as possible!" Jack
Frost shouted at his goblins, waving the
mask around again.

At that moment, Kirsty leaned forward
and snatched the mask right out of Jack
Frost's hand.

Jack Frost spun to face her. "Stop that girl!" he roared. All the goblins ran forward as Kirsty darted back into the passageway.

Rachel pulled the door closed behind Kirsty just as Jack Frost lifted his wand.

"This will stop them," said Flora as she sent a cloud of magical fairy dust toward the wall. The sparkles framed the door with a glittering outline, sealing it firmly shut.

Then Rachel, Kirsty, and Flora hurried off down the secret passage.

A few moments later, they were back in the entrance hall.

"That was close!" Rachel exclaimed. "I'm sure Jack Frost was about to cast a horrible spell!"

"You did fantastically, Kirsty," Flora added. "Now let's get the magic mask back to Lindsay as quickly as we can."

"There are Lindsay and Robert," Kirsty murmured, pointing across the room. "Don't they look great?"

Rachel nodded. "They look
like the king and queen of
the ball," she said with
a smile.

Lindsay was dressed in
a beautiful ballgown
covered by beads and
sparkling jewels. Robert
was wearing an embroidered
jacket, pants, and a shirt
with a ruffly white collar.
They both wore gold
crowns.

"Lindsay!" Kirsty called.
"We found your mask."

Lindsay stared down
her nose at the girls.
"How dare you
approach me in

such a rude manner?"
she snapped haughtily.
"Be gone, immediately!"
Rachel and Kirsty
stared at each
other in confusion.
"It's OK," Flora
whispered from Kirsty's
shoulder. "Lindsay's
acting like a real queen
because the mask isn't
back in its rightful
place yet."
Quickly, Kirsty pressed
the magic mask
into Lindsay's hand.
Lindsay blinked a
couple of times and
then seemed to wake

up, almost as though she'd been in a trance. Robert and all the other guests did the same.

"Thank you, girls," Lindsay said gratefully, as Rachel and Kirsty glanced at each other in relief. "I'm so glad you found my mask." She shook her head as

she held the mask up in the air. "I felt so strange for a minute there!"

"Now that you're feeling better, we can start the party!" Kirsty said with a smile.

Dressing-up in Fairyland

Lindsay and Robert led the guests to the ballroom, but Rachel and Kirsty hung back until the entrance hall was empty.

"Jack Frost and his goblins will leave now that the magic mask is back in its rightful place," Flora told the girls. "It will make sure the party goes smoothly. You have nothing else to worry about."

"Thank you, Flora," Kirsty said gratefully. "Lindsay and Robert's party will be great now, thanks to you!"

"We did it together!" Flora declared happily.

Suddenly, there was a flash of colored light and a magical rainbow streamed into the entrance hall. Rachel and Kirsty grinned as Bertram, the frog footman, hopped off the end of it.

"Good evening!" Bertram said, bowing low. "The king and queen of Fairyland would like to invite Kirsty and

Rachel to come to their costume party
in the Grand Ballroom."

"Oh, yes please!" the girls said eagerly.

Bertram ushered the girls onto the
end of the rainbow, and Flora flew to
join them. Then they were whisked off
to Fairyland in a whirl of rainbow
colors.

When they arrived at the Fairyland palace, Kirsty and Rachel were thrilled to see everyone waiting for them. The Grand Ballroom had been decorated with glittering white and pink streamers, and all the fairies wore fantastic costumes.

"Welcome!" said King Oberon. He was dressed as King Arthur and Queen Titania was by his side, dressed as Lady Guinevere.

"We want to thank you for making sure all Flora's magic items are back where they belong," the queen told

them. "That means *our* party will be
a success, too. Even Jack Frost and his
goblins are coming tonight. We sent
them an invitation they couldn't refuse!"

Before Rachel and Kirsty could reply,
a magic rainbow streamed in through an
open window, and a scowling Jack Frost
fell onto the floor.

A moment later,
another rainbow
came through
the same window,
and all the
goblins tumbled
off the end
of it as if
they were
sliding out of a chute.
Grumbling, they picked themselves up.

"You must be in costume to attend
our party, Jack Frost," King Oberon said
firmly. "Flora's magic will give you
any outfit you'd like. Now, what will
it be?"

Rachel and Kirsty watched as Jack
Frost frowned in thought.

"I want to be a pirate king!" he declared at last.

Flora fluttered over to him and waved her wand over his head. Sparkling fairy dust instantly transformed Jack Frost into a pirate king, complete with an eyepatch, gold hoop earring, and big black boots— plus a huge pirate hat!

Rachel and Kirsty grinned to see that the goblins were wearing pirate costumes, too. Some of them even had peg legs, or parrots on their shoulders.

Looking very pleased with himself, Jack Frost strode off toward the tables of party food. "Come along, me hearties!" he shouted, just like a pirate.

"Aye-aye, Captain!" the goblins yelled. They followed Jack Frost, waving their swords enthusiastically.

"Don't worry," Flora told the girls, "the swords aren't sharp at all." She looked down at her mermaid costume. "It's a new party, so I need a new

outfit!" she remarked. Rachel and Kirsty watched as Flora waved her wand above her head. Purple and black sparkles surrounded her for a moment, and her mermaid tail changed into a frilly, black dress.

A large, pointed hat appeared on her head, and suddenly she was hovering in the air on a broomstick.

"You're a witch!" Kirsty cried.

"A very friendly-looking witch," Rachel pointed out. She and Kirsty laughed as a tiny black cat appeared at the end of the broomstick, meowing loudly.

Flora grinned at them and fluttered down from her broomstick. The broom and the cat immediately followed her.

"Thank you for coming, girls," said Queen Titania, "but it's time for you to return to McKersey Castle."

Rachel and Kirsty gave Flora a big hug. Then all the fairies gathered around in their wonderful costumes to wave to the girls as the queen lifted her wand.

"Good-bye!" called Rachel and Kirsty

as they were whisked away on a cloud of fairy magic.

Almost instantly, Rachel and Kirsty found themselves outside the ballroom at McKersey Castle. They could hear music

playing inside, and people talking and laughing.

"It sounds like the party's going well," Rachel remarked, pushing open the doors as the girls walked through.

But Kirsty wasn't listening. She was staring down at the harps they'd left on the table earlier that day. "Rachel," she said softly, "our harps aren't cardboard anymore. The fairies must have made them *real*!" She ran her fingers over the silver strings and four clear, melodic notes rang out.

Rachel smiled dreamily at her own harp. "Isn't fairy magic *wonderful*?"

she said, peeking into the ballroom
where people were dancing beneath the
glittering chandeliers.

"Fairy magic is the best!" Kirsty
agreed happily, as the girls went into the
ballroom to join the party.

SPECIAL EDITION

Don't miss Rachel and Kirsty's other
magical adventures!

Take a look at this special sneak peek of

Party in Fairyland

"Race you to that tidepool, Kirsty!"
Rachel Walker yelled to her best friend,
Kirsty Tate.

"You're on!" Kirsty replied.

Laughing, the two girls ran across the
beach. Rachel reached the pool first, but
Kirsty was right behind her.

"Your gran is lucky to live in
Leamouth!" Rachel panted, gazing
around the sandy bay. "It's so pretty."

Kirsty nodded. Leamouth was a little fishing village with winding streets and a harbor filled with boats. Kirsty's gran lived in a cottage on the cliff, near the beach.

"I always have fun here," said Kirsty. "I'm glad you could come this time, too."

"Thanks for inviting me!" Rachel replied.

The two girls wandered down to the sea. The waves lapped at their flip-flops. As the water slid back, it left a large seashell on the sand right in front of them.

Rachel picked it up. "It's beautiful," she said.

As Kirsty looked, a burst of aquamarine sparkles suddenly fizzed out of the shell, making both girls jump.

Kirsty gasped. "Fairy magic!"

The girls glanced at each other, eyes wide with excitement. Their friendship with the fairies was a very special secret.

Soft music and the faint tinkle of bells floated out of the shell. Quickly, Rachel held it up so she and Kirsty could listen.

"Hello, girls," said a small voice.

Rachel grinned at Kirsty. "It's the fairy queen!" she exclaimed.

"We'd like to invite you to a special beach party — a luau — to celebrate summer," the queen said. "If you'd like to come, just place the shell on the sand right now. We hope you can join us. . . ." The queen's voice faded away.

With a quick glance around to make sure nobody was watching, Rachel

placed the seashell on the sand.
Immediately, a dazzling rainbow sprang
from the shell. Its colors were bright in
the sunshine.

"Let's go, Kirsty!" Rachel whispered.

Kirsty nodded, and the girls stepped
onto the rainbow. As soon as they did,
they were whisked away in a whirl of
fairy magic.

When the sparkles vanished, the girls
had been magically transformed into
fairies. They were in Fairyland, standing
on a beautiful sandy beach next to a
glittering turquoise sea. The beach was
crowded with fairies enjoying the luau.

As the girls stepped away from the
rainbow, their fairy friends rushed to
greet them, including King Oberon and
Queen Titania.

"We're so glad you could come, girls," the king said kindly.

"A party wouldn't be the same without you," the queen added.

"Thank you for inviting us," Rachel and Kirsty chorused.

"Come and dance!" called Jade the Disco Fairy.

Laughing, Rachel and Kirsty joined Jade. Meanwhile, they could see another fairy conducting the musicians, and other fairies cooking food on a barbecue.

"The tide's coming in," Rachel remarked to Jade as the waves crept further up the beach. "Will the party be over soon?"

Jade shook her head. "No, we'll be fine as long as we stay above Party Rock," she replied, pointing to a large boulder nearby. "But Shannon the Ocean Fairy can explain it better than I can."

A nearby fairy turned and smiled at the girls. She wore a peach-colored skirt, a top made of aqua ribbons, and a glittering starfish clip in her hair.

"Hi, girls," Shannon greeted them. "Jade's right. The sea never comes past Party Rock, so we can enjoy the party all day long!"

"Great!" Rachel said happily.

A little while later, the girls were still having fun dancing with their fairy friends when the music suddenly stopped. Everyone turned to see what had happened.

"Listen, please," called Shannon the Ocean Fairy. "I'm afraid that the sea is coming in too far!"

She pointed her wand at Party Rock and everyone gasped in surprise. The water was splashing around the base of the rock, and the level was still rising!

"The water never comes in this far," Shannon declared anxiously. "Something's wrong!"

RAINBOW magic™

There's Magic in Every Series!

The Rainbow Fairies
The Weather Fairies
The Jewel Fairies
The Pet Fairies
The Fun Day Fairies
The Petal Fairies
The Dance Fairies
The Music Fairies
The Sports Fairies
The Party Fairies
The Ocean Fairies

Read them all!

■ SCHOLASTIC

www.scholastic.com
www.rainbowmagiconline.com

HIT entertainment

RMFAIRY

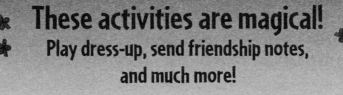

These activities are magical!

Play dress-up, send friendship notes, and much more!

■ SCHOLASTIC

www.scholastic.com

www.rainbowmagiconline.com

HiT entertainment

RMACTIV3

Perfectly Princess

Don't miss these royal adventures!

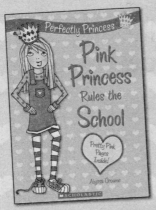

Printed on colored pages!

www.scholastic.com
www.rainbowmagiconline.com

HiT entertainment

DANCEF